• I AM READING •
ALBERT'S RACCOON

KAREN WALLACE

Illustrated by
GRAHAM PERCY

For Henry – K.W.
For Gabriel – G.P.

KINGFISHER

An imprint of Kingfisher Publications Plc
New Penderel House, 283-288 High Holborn
London WC1V 7HZ

First published by Kingfisher 2001
4 6 8 10 9 7 5 3
3TR/0602/TWP/GRS/115GKBMA

Text copyright © Karen Wallace 2001
Illustrations copyright © Graham Percy 2001

The moral right of the author and illustrator has been asserted.

A CIP catalogue record for this book
is available from the British Library.

ISBN 0 7534 0489 3

Printed in Singapore

Contents

Chapter One

One day Albert came home from
school and saw a large wooden
box sitting on the doorstep.
It was from his Uncle Fred.
"Oh dear," said Albert's mother.
"The last time Uncle Fred came
to stay he left two snakes under
his bed and a giant bat hanging
on the back of the bedroom door."

Her face went
white just thinking
about it.

Albert's father rolled his eyes.
"And the time before that, he
left a hippopotamus in the pond."

They all looked at the box again.

There was a letter pinned to

its side.

Dear Albert,
Please look after Rocky.
He eats frogs, chicken legs,
crabs, clams, apples, nuts,
beetles and lizards.
I have gone to help a bear
with a sore head.
Love, Uncle Fred

Albert opened the box.

A small black and white animal

with a striped tail climbed out.

It looked like a furry burglar.

It was a raccoon.

"Wow!" cried Albert.

"Oh dear," said his mother.

"Oh no," said his father.

"Churr-churr," said Rocky the

raccoon.

7

For the rest of the day Albert and
Rocky played together.

They hunted for apples.

They cracked nuts.

They looked everywhere for lizards.

Soon they were the best of friends.

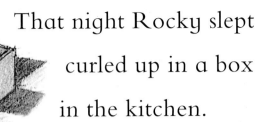

That night Rocky slept
curled up in a box
in the kitchen.

That night Albert was
so excited he could hardly sleep.

He was excited because he was going
to visit his father's sweet factory the
next day.

But most of all he was excited because
he had a brand new, wonderful pet!

Chapter Two

Early the next morning a terrible
scream came from the kitchen.
Albert jumped out of bed
and ran down the stairs.
Albert's mother was standing
in the middle of the kitchen.
It looked like something out
of a strange dream.

The toaster was making spaghetti.

The pasta machine was making toast.

The fruit juice maker was peeling
potatoes.
And the washing machine was
cooking scrambled eggs for breakfast.

Albert's father walked into the
kitchen. Rocky opened one eye . . .
then quickly pretended to be asleep.
Albert's father looked at
Albert's mother.
Albert's mother looked at Albert.
Then everyone looked at
Albert's raccoon.

Rocky kept his eyes tight shut.

But everyone knew that raccoons

love fiddling with things.

And everyone could see the bits of

washing machine he was trying to

hide under his tail . . .

"That raccoon is not staying in
my house!" cried Albert's mother.
"What are we going to do?"
said Albert's father.
"I'll phone the Raccoon Protection
League. They can collect him
today," said Albert's mother.
"Churr-churr!" said Rocky.

"I don't want Rocky to go!"

cried Albert.

"Don't worry, dear," said his mother.

"We'll get you another pet. A puppy

or a kitten, perhaps."

But Albert wasn't listening.

He was making a plan.

Chapter Three

Behind the kitchen door was Albert's old panda bear backpack.

It didn't look much like a raccoon, but his plan might just work.

Albert picked up Rocky and put him inside his shiny *new* backpack.

"Don't make a noise," whispered Albert. Rocky's bright eyes glittered. It was as if he understood every word.

Then Albert put the old panda bear backpack into Rocky's box and curled it up to look as if it was asleep.

Albert couldn't help grinning to himself. The Raccoon Protection League would get a big surprise when they arrived to collect Rocky!

Ten minutes later

Albert and his father set off for the

sweet factory.

"Today is a very important day

at the factory, Albert," said his father.

"Why?" asked Albert.

"Mr Caramel Chew is coming, so

nothing must go wrong."

Albert felt his face go red.

"Who's Mr Caramel Chew?"
he asked.

"Mr Caramel Chew owns sweet
shops all over the world," explained
Albert's father. "If he likes my sweets,
he'll buy loads and loads of them."

"Churr-churr," said Rocky from
inside Albert's backpack.

"I beg your pardon?" said Albert's
father.

Albert went even redder.

"Er, er . . . I'm sure Mr Chew will
love your sweets," he said quickly.
At that moment they drove
through the factory gates.

Chapter Four

The telephone was ringing when
Albert and his father walked into
the sweet factory.

"I won't be a minute," said Albert's
father. "Don't touch anything!"
Albert grinned. The factory was his
favourite place in the whole world.
It was full of machines that whistled
and rumbled and rattled.

At one end of the factory six huge beaters twirled round and round in six tubs full of sticky sweet mixture.

At the other end of the factory the sweet mixture was baked in a giant oven.

Then it was cut into all kinds of shapes
and sizes by a special chopping machine.

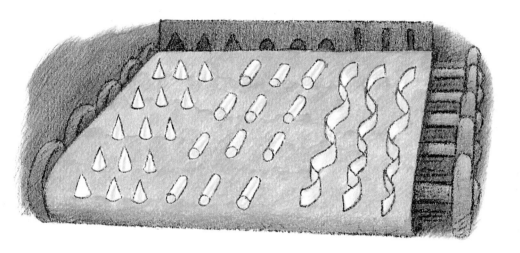

Finally, all the sweets were covered
with different coloured coatings.

Bong!

Splatter!

The sweets poured out of a huge silver
tube onto an enormous tasting tray.
That was Albert's favourite part.

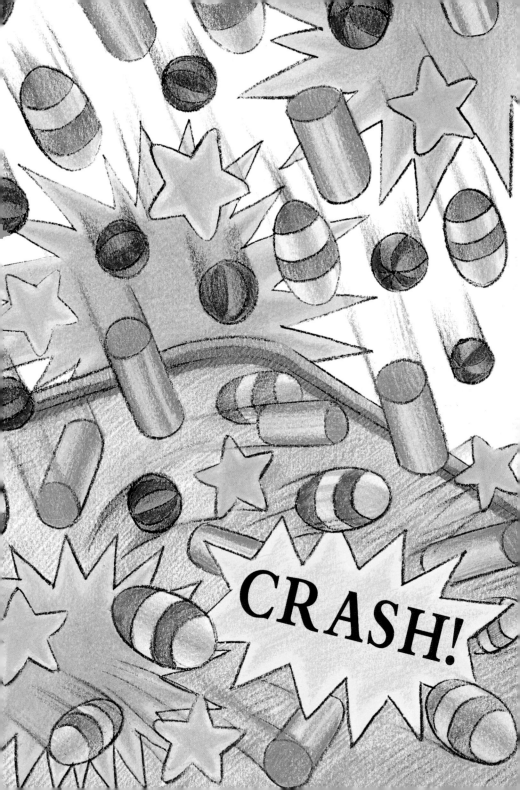

Albert lifted his backpack off his shoulders.

"I'll show you around if you promise not to touch anything," he whispered to Rocky.

But when he opened the backpack, his stomach turned to ice.

Rocky had disappeared!

Chapter Five

BANG!

"Albert!" cried his father.

He ran from his office through a

snowstorm of marshmallows.

He ducked as thousands of jelly

babies shot through the air.

"I asked you not to touch—"

But he never finished his sentence.

Through the control room
window he saw a black and white
furry animal sitting in front of a
panel of levers and lights.
It was Rocky the raccoon –
and he was having the best
fun ever!
Suddenly the machines went
crazy and made a noise they
had never made before.
Albert gulped.
Albert's father's eyes went as big
as saucers.
Just then the factory door
swung open . . .

"Good morning!" said a deep, smooth voice.

A man wearing a brown and white suit and carrying a gold-topped cane walked in through the factory door. "Mr Caramel Chew, at your service," he said.

Albert's father's face
turned the colour
of icing sugar.

"Aren't you expecting
me?" said Mr Caramel
Chew in a puzzled
voice.

Albert's father opened
his mouth, but no
words came out.

Albert looked at Rocky.
Rocky looked back.
His eyes twinkled.
Suddenly Albert
knew everything
would be all right.

"Of course we're
expecting you!"
he said quickly.
"And we have
some wonderful
sweets to
show you!"

"We do?" said Albert's father in a hollow voice.

"Of course we do," said Albert.

Mr Caramel Chew looked from one to the other.

He flipped open his notebook.

"Excellent!" he said. "Show me the way!"

Chapter Six

Albert, Albert's father and
Mr Caramel Chew stood in front
of the giant tasting tray.

It was empty.

"Never mind," said Mr Caramel
Chew smoothly. "I'll come back
another day."

He snapped his notebook shut.

"Please wait!" cried Albert.

He gulped and looked up at Rocky in the control room. "I'm sure *something* will happen."

Albert's father rolled his eyes. Suddenly there was a whizz and a whirr and a clatter from the sweet-making machine.

"Goodness me!" cried Mr Caramel Chew. "Something *is* happening!"

WHOOOOOSH!

A waterfall of sweets
poured out of the huge
silver tube and crashed
onto the tasting tray.
They were the
strangest-looking sweets
you could ever imagine.
There were no gobstoppers
or minty drops.
There were no liquorice sticks
or chocolate twirls.
There were no fruit gums or
toffees or lemon sherbets.

Instead there were sugary green frogs and chewy chicken legs. There were frosted pink crabs and smooth chocolate clams. There were peppermint lizards and crunchy orange beetles.

They were just the sort of sweets
a raccoon might like to eat!
Albert gasped and went bright red.
Whatever would Mr Caramel
Chew say?

"Brilliant!" said Mr Caramel Chew.

He clapped his hands and danced

around his cane.

"Your sweets are absolutely

BRILLIANT!" he cried.

"I've never seen anything

like them!"

Mr Caramel Chew grabbed

Albert's father by the hand.

"Congratulations, my dear sir!

I'll buy everything you have –

and I'll order a million more!"

"A million?" croaked Albert's father.

Mr Caramel Chew threw back

his head and laughed.

"All right! TWO million!" he said.

At that moment Rocky the raccoon
scampered across the floor
and jumped into Albert's arms.

"Goodness gracious!" cried
Mr Caramel Chew. He peered into
Rocky's clever eyes.

"Why, it looks like a raccoon!"
Albert's father patted Albert's
shoulders and tickled Rocky's ears.
"This isn't a raccoon," he said
proudly. "This is a small, furry,
sweet-making genius."

He laughed and ruffled Albert's hair.

"And he belongs to my son, Albert!"

Albert looked up.

"Does that mean I can keep him

forever?" he whispered.

"Forever," said Albert's father

with a smile.

About the Author and Illustrator

Karen Wallace is an award-winning writer and has published over 70 books for children. She was born in Canada where she lived with her family in a log cabin. "We had friends with a pet raccoon. It lived in their house," says Karen. "The only problem was that the raccoon took everything apart at night – so they had to build him a little home in the garden. That was the raccoon I was thinking about when I wrote this story."

Graham Percy was born and brought up in New Zealand. He came to London to study at the Royal College of Art and has illustrated many books for children. Graham has never met a real raccoon but he says, "Sometimes my studio looks as if Rocky has been in there, playing with my paints and knocking pencils all over my desk!"

Here are some **I Am Reading** books for you to enjoy:

ALLIGATOR TAILS AND CROCODILE CAKES
Nicola Moon & Andy Ellis

BARN PARTY
Claire O'Brien & Tim Archbold

THE GIANT POSTMAN
Sally Grindley & Wendy Smith

GRANDAD'S DINOSAUR
Brough Girling & Stephen Dell

JJ RABBIT AND THE MONSTER
Nicola Moon & Ant Parker

JOE LION'S BIG BOOTS
Kara May & Jonathan Allen

JUST MABEL
Frieda Wishinsky & Sue Heap

KIT'S CASTLE
Chris Powling & Anthony Lewis

MISS WIRE AND THE THREE KIND MICE
Ian Whybrow & Emma Chichester Clark

MR COOL
Jacqueline Wilson & Stephen Lewis

MRS HIPPO'S PIZZA PARLOUR
Vivian French & Clive Scruton

PRINCESS ROSA'S WINTER
Judy Hindley & Margaret Chamberlain

WATCH OUT, WILLIAM
Kady MacDonald Denton